Pigín of Howth

For my grandchildren,
Cian, Sadhbh, Saoirse, Kate and Harry

Pigín
of Howth

Kathleen Watkins

Illustrated by Margaret Anne Suggs

Gill Books

Gill Books
Hume Avenue
Park West
Dublin 12
www.gillbooks.ie

Gill Books is an imprint of M.H. Gill & Co.

978 07171 6972 6

Edited by Síne Quinn
Printed by L.E.G.O. SpA, Italy

This book is typeset in 20 on 25pt Bembo Schoolbook.

The paper used in this book comes from the wood pulp of
managed forests. For every tree felled, at least one tree is
planted, thereby renewing natural resources.

A CIP catalogue record for this book is available from the
British Library.

5 4 3 2

Pigs Can't Fly, but They Can Swim!

I t was a beautiful
sunny morning
as Pigín looked out the
window of his little house beside the
GAA playing fields on the Hill of
Howth. He picked up his mobile phone
and called his friend Sammy Seal.

'Hello, Sammy,' he said, 'it's the perfect day for a
picnic on Ireland's Eye.'

'Yes, it is. Come on down when you're ready,
Pigín,' Sammy said. 'And don't forget your life jacket.'

Just as Pigín arrived at the harbour, groups
of people were walking down the pier.

'Well, would you look at that,' said one
of them. 'A piglet in a life jacket with a
phone and a flute! Am I dreaming?'

'That's Pigín,' the Harbour Master said, who was standing nearby. 'He lives here in Howth and is a fine piglet indeed.'

'Hello there,' Pigín said, smiling at the man. 'I live here on the peninsula. I like the word PEN-IN-SU-LA.'

And off he trotted down the pier to meet Sammy Seal and his four brothers: Sean, Seamus, Seoirse and Shane. The little piglet was very excited because the seals had promised to give him a swimming lesson.

When he saw the five big seals in the water, Pigín climbed
down the ladder and leaped onto Sammy's back.

'Ah! VERY cold splashes!' he said, and gave a loud squeal and a shiver.

'Not at all …' Sammy replied.

'All very well for you,' Pigín said. 'You live in it!'

They moved out of the mouth of Howth Harbour with Sammy's
four brothers swimming in pairs behind them. The pod of seals moved
quickly and gracefully in the water. Pigín held on tight to Sammy, but
managed to wave a trotter to say farewell to the Harbour Master.

'Oh, look!' Sammy said. 'The children are doing a sailing course.'

'There's Sadhbh, Nanakit's granddaughter,' Pigín said. 'Oh, no – she
has capsized!'

'Don't worry, she could not be safer,' Sammy said.

'She is wearing her life jacket and the crash boat is there to pick her up.'

'She is a good swimmer too,' Pigín said. 'You must teach me to swim
when we get to the island.'

After a few minutes they arrived on Ireland's Eye, where Sammy and his four brothers helped Pigín with his swimming lesson. At first Pigín was scared, but he knew he could do it. He took off his life jacket, climbed off Sammy's back and moved his trotters as fast as he could.

Pigín made dreadful snorting noises as the sea water got up his snout and into his ears, but he kept trying. Pigs can't fly, but they can swim, he thought as he began to swim faster and faster. The seals all whistled and clapped. They were delighted to see the little piglet swimming in the sea.

'I'm learning fast! This is wonderful. I love it, especially floating on my back,' he said, while blowing a spray of sea water out of his mouth.

'Can I dive off the rocks?' Pigín asked the seals.

'As often as you like!' the seals said in unison.

Pigín jumped and dived many times. Then the seals gave him a water ballet display. He had never seen anything like it before.

'It's called synchronised swimming,' Sammy said. The seals practise their synchronised swimming every day.

Pigín took photos with his mobile phone. 'Nanakit will want to see these,' he said.

When the seals finished their display the little piglet played the flute for them and danced to music on his phone, lifting his trotters high off the ground. The seals were delighted. They clapped and cheered and swam in circles with delight.

'We are so lucky to be here having such a good time,' Pigín said. 'We'll have to come again soon.'

They had a delicious picnic and then they all felt very, very sleepy. They lay on the rocks and closed their eyes. The only sounds to be heard were the waves washing up on the shore and an aeroplane overhead.

The sound of the plane woke Pigín. 'There's the green bird on its way to Dublin Airport,' he said. 'And I'm going to be on one soon!'

'Tell me more, Pigín,' Sammy said, stretching after his nap.

'I'm going to London on my holidays –'

Pigín's story was interrupted by the noise of the fishing boats coming home.

'Quickly, Sean, Seamus, Seoirse and Shane,' Sammy called, 'let's go back to Howth Harbour for some fish!'

When they arrived at the harbour, Kevin from Nicky's Plaice rang a bell and came out of the shop with buckets of fish heads and tails. The seals had a feast. Dozens of people gathered at the edge of the pier to look at the seals, including some of the children from the sailing course.

Pigín said thank you to Sammy and his brothers. 'That was the best day I ever had. Thank you so much.'

Pigín could hardly hear his own voice because of the deafening noise of the excited and greedy seagulls overhead.

When he turned to go he saw something on the ground. It was a phone.

'Oh, excuse me, sir. Is this yours?' Pigín asked a man in a red jacket standing beside him.

The man turned around. 'It must have slipped out of my pocket,' he said. 'Thank you very much, Pigín. What a great fella you are. I'm lucky that you found it.'

'It's a pleasure, sir,' said Pigín, and off he trotted to get on the little train that would take him to Nanakit's house near the Baily Lighthouse.

On the way, Pigín wrote a thank you note to the seals. I could send a text, he thought, but it is always nice to receive a note. He called his friend Sally Seagull on his mobile phone, who flew down and took the note in her beak to deliver it to the seals at the harbour.

Pigín was tired when he arrived at Nanakit's cottage.

'Your hair is lovely, Nanakit,' he said, smiling at his good friend.

'I got it done in the village earlier,' she said. 'Come in and tell me about your day. You can stay the night, if you like. I have a bed made up for you.'

Pigín sat down in one of Nanakit's big, cosy armchairs and looked at the tea table she had prepared for him. There was a beautiful tablecloth and napkins, with delicate china cups and delicious things to eat.

'This is perfect, Nanakit! Thank you.'

'I'll just put the kettle on,' she said, 'and you can tell me about your day.'

Nanakit came back with the teapot. 'We will leave it there for a moment,' she said.

There was no reply.

Nanakit looked at Pigín fast asleep in the
armchair with a great big smile on his face.
She covered him with her best blue blanket
and sat down to pour herself a nice
cup of tea.

Pigín's Magical Midnight Adventure

Pigín's mobile phone rang. It was his friend the Fairy Queen. 'Pigín, I thought your Dublin jersey was a bit worn,' she said. 'I've made you a new one.'

'Really? Thank you. That's great!' said Pigín. 'The Badger of Ballsbridge and I are going to see the Dubs at their training session today, so I'll wear it for that.'

The fairies have lovely houses in the tree trunks behind Howth Castle where they make all of Pigín's clothes. They even send orders to Magee of Donegal to get tweed for Pigín's warm winter jackets.

'That's a perfect Dubs jersey!' Pigín said. 'Thank you so much.'

'Come back again in the evening on your way home,' the Fairy Queen said. 'We have a surprise for you and Badger.'

Pigín thanked the fairies again and went off to the DART station wearing his smart outfit.

Badger got on the DART at Sandymount. The station
master put out the ramp and Badger climbed up.
Pigín could not believe his eyes when he met
Badger at Connolly station.

'You've painted your stripes blue for the Dubs,' he said.
'Well done, Badger. You're a real sport.'

The friends then got a bus to Parnell Park to
watch the Dublin GAA teams training.

'Look at how hard they work,' Pigín said. 'Lots of stretches and exercises before they even touch the ball.'

'UP THE DUBS!' Badger shouted.

'COME ON THE DUBS!' Pigín roared.

Both hurling and football teams were in training. The teams were amused to see a piglet and a badger watching them from the side-lines and wearing the Dublin colours.

'Which game do you like best?' Pigín asked.

'Hurling,' Badger replied. 'It is so fast.'

'I love both,' Pigín said, as he took photos of the players on his phone. 'Let's have our picnic, and then we can go home to my place. Don't forget we are going to see the fairies later.'

On the way home, Pigín and Badger peeped in the windows of the school in Howth to see the children learning to play the violin.

'They have only started to learn and they are doing very well. They look like they are working hard at it, but there's a lot of scraping in the beginning,' the little piglet said, covering his ears with his trotters.

'To be good at anything you have to work at it,' Badger said, as he stood up taller to catch another glimpse of the violin teacher demonstrating a new note to little Saoirse, Nanakit's granddaughter.

Off they went to Pigín's house. Pigín and Badger had a shower, and Badger washed off the Dublin blue colour from the white stripes on his furry head.

When the pair were washed and dressed, Pigín said: 'Now let's go and visit the fairies.'

What a sight Pigín and Badger saw when they arrived behind the castle! There in the moonlight, eight magnificently dressed fairies sat in a circle playing golden knee-harps. Pigín's eyes widened. He was entranced. The fairies seemed to shimmer from the tip of their glittering wings to the heels of their dainty shoes. Even their gossamer dresses and lace tights glistened in the moonlight.

'What an amazing sight,' Pigín said, 'and what a beautiful sound.'

'The best I have ever heard!' Badger said. 'And look at their outfits – such lovely party dresses.'

Badger sighed in wonder: 'It's magical, that's just what it is. Magical!'

'There's more magic,' the Fairy Queen said. 'Look up.'

Pigín and Badger looked up.

'I can't believe it,' Pigín said. 'It's a magic carpet. A real magic carpet!'

The colourful carpet hovered above the ground.

'We'll never get up there!' Badger cried, shaking his head.

'Yes, you will!' the fairies chorused. They fixed wings on Pigín's and Badger's backs and up they flew onto the carpet. The fairies joined them and they all took off for the Baily Lighthouse.

'I've never seen such a view of the peninsula,' Pigín said. 'The moon is lighting up the whole place. We can see everything. Kate and Harry are having a sleepover in Nanakit's tonight. They don't even know we are up here!'

They gazed at the twinkling lights on Howth Head and looked out at the moonlit bay. They spotted the lighthouse with its strong light that guides the boats. The fairies brought the carpet down beside the lighthouse.

When the magic carpet landed with a light thud, they stepped off and looked around.

They heard a stern voice behind them: 'Good evening, can I help you?' asked Peter, the chief lighthouse keeper, who was on night duty.

When Peter shone his torch on the group of friends, he was glad to see that it was the fairies with his old friend Pigín and the famous Badger of Ballsbridge.

Peter brought the group inside and they climbed up the steep steps to see the light. The sea looked silvery as it glistened in the moonlight. Dublin Bay looked wonderful.

The fairies invited Peter to join them for a delicious supper.

'Just wait until I tell Nanakit about this, Peter,' Pigín said. 'She'll be glad we met you.'

After a while it was time to go home.

'I'm really sleepy,' Badger said with a great big yawn.

'Me too,' Pigín said, also yawning.

They thanked Peter before they all got onto the magic carpet again. The fairies sang them to sleep as they floated home over the Hill of Howth. Pigín, Badger and the younger fairies, who were curled up beside each other, were all sleeping soundly on the carpet.

The Fairy Queen used her magic to ensure the carpet moved slowly and gracefully, and didn't make any sharp twists or turns as she guided it back to Pigín's house.

The next morning Pigín and Badger woke up to find themselves in Pigín's bedroom.

'How did we get here?' Badger asked, yawning. He spotted his suitcase open at the foot of the spare bed. It was packed with a new pair of clothes and his toothbrush. He guessed the fairies must have put it there. 'They think of everything!'

'It's magic,' Pigín said, smiling at his friend. 'That is what it is. Magic! Fairies can do anything with a magic wand. Let's get up and have a nice big breakfast before we start another day.'

A Day
to Wear a
Top Hat

Pigín was very excited because Nanakit had got him tickets for the Dublin Horse Show. Early one morning, the little piglet raced up to Nanakit's house as fast as his trotters would carry him to collect the tickets.

When Pigín was sitting in Nanakit's front room, Cian raced in the door.
'Come on out for a bit of football?' he asked.

Pigín was delighted to see Nanakit's grandson. Though he was tired
from running up to Nanakit's house, the thought of a kick around outside
made the little piglet leap out of his armchair with excitement.

Out they went and Pigín gave the ball a great big kick – so big that it
went over the cliff!

'Wow, Pigín, that was a mighty kick!' Cian said.

'Fine trotters indeed!' Pigín replied.

'Let's go get it,' Cian said, and they stumbled down the cliff right onto a very muddy path.

The ball had disappeared. 'Forget the ball,' Pigín said, 'let's play in the mud!' And he dived onto the path.

'Yippee, this is fun!' Cian said, as he joined Pigín in the soft, brown, wet, dirty, sticky mud.

They shrieked and giggled and rolled around until they were covered in mud.

'We look like two big bars of melted chocolate. Let's show Nanakit,' Pigín said, as they climbed back up the cliff to the garden.

'She might not recognise us,' Cian replied.

They fell about laughing at the sound of the mud squelching as they walked back to the garden.

Nanakit was very cross when she realised what they had done. She ran out the back door.

'Stay right there, you naughty boys!' she said as she hosed them down. Cian and Pigín squealed with laughter and shrieked when the cold water washed them down.

'Come in now and shower,' Nanakit said, wrapping them in big, warm bath towels.

The pair emerged from their showers for their tea.

'We're starving!' Cian said, as they sat into Nanakit's big, cosy armchairs.

'Now I'll make more fresh tea,' she said, shaking her head and smiling.

What the little piglet didn't know was that the fairies had a surprise for their friend. They had just finished making more beautiful clothes for Pigín, including an outfit for the Dublin Horse Show. They had also made a top hat for Pigín and his friend, the Badger of Ballsbridge.

'Please put them in a big parcel and go to Pigín's house,' the Fairy Queen said, placing the folded suit and top hats in a box.

When the parcel was ready, she said the magic words: 'Gilly, gilly,' and sprinkled it with magic powder. 'Oofledust, oofledust,' she said, and suddenly the parcel developed arms and legs!

'Yippee!' the fairies cried, as the parcel ran out the door to deliver itself to Pigín.

Pigín was thrilled with his new clothes. 'Wow! Two top hats for the Horse Show,' he exclaimed.

He sent a text message to Badger: 'We'll go on the DART on Thursday to see the horse jumping. Nanakit has given me two tickets, and we might get to see the President of Ireland!'

Early on Thursday morning, Pigín went down to Nicky's Plaice at the pier to get a side of smoked salmon for the President.

'Good morning, Kevin,' he said. 'Please may I have the best smoked salmon in the house? It is a gift for the President. Badger and I are going to meet him at the Horse Show. How much will that be?'

'Please give it as a gift to the President with my compliments!' Kevin said.

'Oh, thank you, Kevin,' Pigín said, 'that is so kind and generous of you.'

And off he went to the DART. It was packed, but Pigín was pleased to see children giving their seats to older people and gentlemen giving up their seats to ladies. A gentleman never sits when a lady is standing, thought Pigín.

The little piglet stood out in his top hat and tails. He chuckled to himself when he remembered how muddy he and Cian had been the day before.

At Bayside station, a lady got on with a little black and white dog. Pigín smiled at her and gave her his seat. Suddenly the lady got the dog to do tricks.

'Roly poly!' she said, and the little dog rolled all around the floor of the DART.

'Dance!' she said, and the dog danced up and down the carriage.

'Sing!' she said, and he made a very strange sound indeed. The little dog did his best.

'Hide!' she said, and he dived under the seat.

It was all very exciting and everybody clapped.

'I never thought a trip on the DART could be such fun!' Pigín said, looking around.

Soon the DART arrived at Sandymount station. Badger was there to meet Pigín.

'Pigín, you look sensational. What's in the box?' Badger asked.

He gasped when he saw the elegant top hat the fairies had made him. Badger was over the moon.

'And what's in the parcel?' Badger asked.

'Smoked salmon for the President,' Pigín said proudly. 'I hope we get to meet him.'

The show grounds were packed with people, and the Army Band was playing on the Band Stand.

'Look at those lovely army uniforms,' Pigín said. 'They have two flute players. Maybe I should have brought mine.'

'Look over there!' Badger said. 'It's a group of ladies all lined up. They are going to pick the best-dressed lady.'

The ladies smiled and waved when they noticed the smartly dressed piglet and badger.

'I want the lady in the blue to win,' Pigín said. 'She is wearing my favourite colour.'

'She even has blue shoes to match,' Badger said. 'She's gorgeous.'

Just then the winner was announced.

'It's Emer O'Driscoll from Cork!' the man on the stand said, as the lady in blue stepped forward to accept a big bunch of flowers and lots of parcels.

'I just knew she would be the winner,' Pigín said. 'Now let's go and see the horse jumping.'

As they got to their seats the President arrived. Pigín helped Badger up onto the seat beside him.

'These are great seats,' he said. 'They are so close to where the President is sitting.'

All the people clapped and stood up for the President, and then the horse jumping began.

It was such a thrill to see the horses up close. The whole arena was a wonderful sight. The winner was a young man on a horse called Starlet. They had the only clear round with no faults.

'It is my great pleasure to present you with this silver cup,' the President said, as he pinned a big red rosette on the horse's head.

'Come this way, Pigín and Badger,' said a man in a top hat. 'You are going to meet the President.'

'I can't believe it!' Badger said. 'Let's go.'

They were presented to the President, bowing slightly and removing their hats.

'Please accept a gift of smoked salmon from Nicky's Plaice on Howth Pier,' Pigín said, as he gave the parcel to the President.

'Thank you very much,' the President said. 'We are having guests for lunch tomorrow and we shall use it then.'

And so it was time for everyone to go home after such an exciting day.

'It was perfect – the sun shone and it never rained,' Pigín said.

'We had the best of craic!' Badger replied, patting his friend on the back.

'Before you go home on the DART,' Badger added, 'how about a cup of tea and a slice of chocolate cake in my house?'

'That would be lovely,' Pigín said. 'But before we do, let's write three thank you notes. A note to Nanakit for the tickets today, a note to thank the fairies for the top hats and, last but not least, a note to thank Kevin for the salmon. Sally Seagull will deliver them for us.'

'Before you do anything else,' a photographer said, stopping beside them, 'I must take a photo of you both for tomorrow's paper.'

Pigín and Badger stood side by side to have their photograph taken. Then the friends walked happily up the street still looking very fine in their top hats and tails, even after a long and very eventful day.